THE DEATHSTONE

Welcome to the world of
MASK
MOBILE ARMOURED STRIKE KOMMAND.

Imagine a world where there is more to reality than meets the eye. Where illusion and deception team up with man and machine to create a world of sophisticated vehicles and weaponry, manned by agents and counter-agents.

The Deathstone

The MASK mission: to recover a meteor – The Deathstone – with the assistance of young Scott Trakker and his robot companion T-Bob.

The first thrilling **MASK** adventure!

MATT TRAKKER – SPECTRUM

MATT TRAKKER – ULTRA FLASH

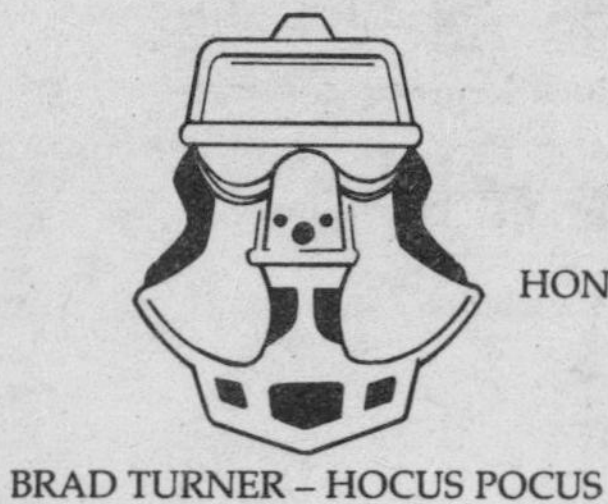

BRAD TURNER – HOCUS POCUS

HONDO MACLEAN – BLASTER

BUDDIE HAWKES – PENETRATOR

BRUCE SATO – LIFTER

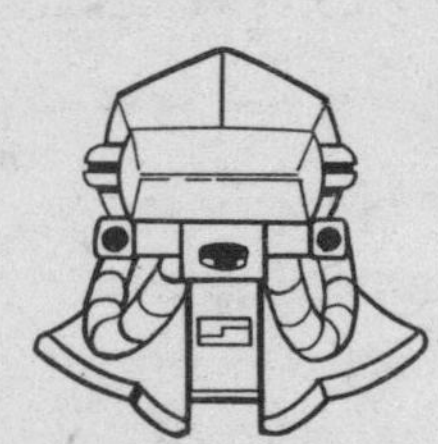

DUSTY HAYES – BACKLASH

ALEX SECTOR – JACKRABBIT

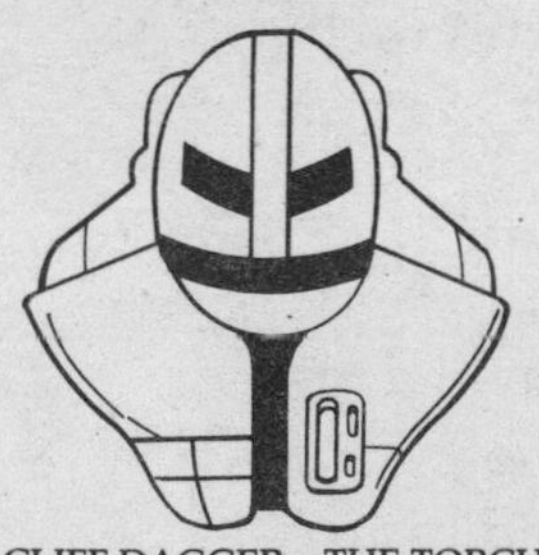

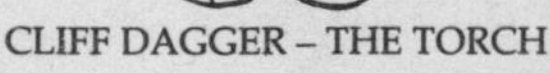

CLIFF DAGGER – THE TORCH

SLY RAX – STILETTO

MILES MAYHEM – VIPER

MASK

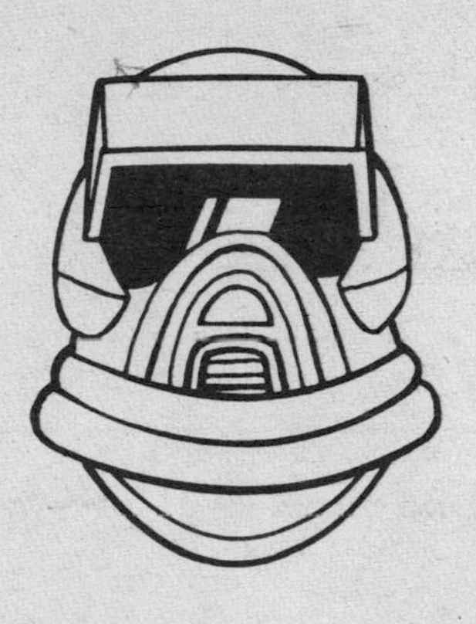

THE DEATHSTONE

novelisation by
Kenneth Harper
Illustrated by Bruce Hogarth

KNIGHT BOOKS
Hodder and Stoughton

With special thanks to Bruce Hogarth and David Lewis Management for their great help and hard work.

First published by Knight Books 1986

British Library C.I.P.
Harper, Kenneth
The deathstone.—(Mask; 1)
I. Title II. Hogarth, Bruce III. Series
823'.914[J] PZ7

ISBN 0-340-39890-6

Printed and bound in Great Britain for Hodder and Stoughton Paperbacks, a division of Hodder and Stoughton Ltd., Mill Road, Dunton Green, Sevenoaks, Kent (Editorial Office: 47 Bedford Square, London WC1B 3DP) by Cox & Wyman Ltd
Photoset by Rowland Phototypesetting Ltd
Bury St Edmunds, Suffolk.

ONE

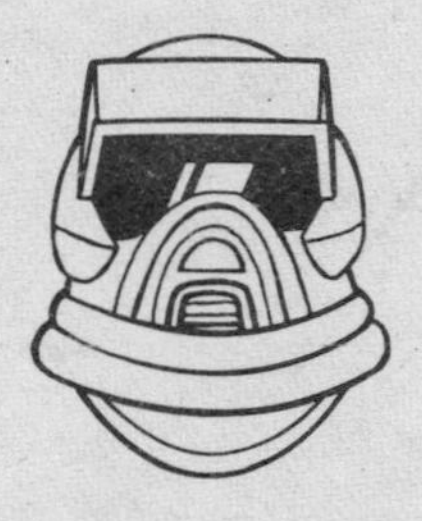

It came from out of nowhere. The large meteor entered the Earth's atmosphere and hurtled downwards with tremendous speed. Flaming through the night sky, it got smaller and smaller as pieces of it fell away and disintegrated. But there was still enough of it left to cause a deep crater when it landed.

The meteor came down in an isolated rocky desert area that was surrounded by high bluffs. It hit the ground with such explosive force that tremors were felt dozens of kilometres away. The night sky was lit up all around. Thick smoke curled upwards from the crater for a long time. There was an acrid smell.

When the smoke finally cleared, the meteor was revealed as a small chunk of rock that was pulsating

with an intense, blue-coloured glow of energy. Around the edge of the crater, plants suddenly began to sprout and flower. Barren land was becoming fertile.

The meteor was creating new life.

Tracking systems had picked it up as soon as it had begun to approach the Earth. Reaction was swift. The Army leapt into action. Troop carriers, jeeps, trucks and other Army vehicles were soon parked in a ring around the crater. Soldiers dressed in radiation clothing watched from a safe distance.

The crater was now overflowing with new, vibrant plant life. A luxuriant garden of rich colours had grown instantly in the middle of the desert. It was full of beauty.

And full of danger.

'Remain one hundred metres from the crater!'

Wearing her radiation suit, Professor Stevens spoke through an electric bullhorn to warn the soldiers all around her.

'The meteor is *extremely* radioactive. Stand clear!'

Her voice was electronically distorted and it was impossible to tell that it belonged to a young woman. Professor Stevens, a top scientist, reinforced her message.

'Your suits will not protect you if you go any closer!'

But the soldiers were no longer listening to her.

Another sound filled their ears. A loud whirring noise that built to a crescendo. The whole area was suddenly engulfed in blinding strobe lights that seemed to come from above. Fear spread quickly as the sound became more deafening and the light more dazzling.

Even the vehicles responded.

Their horns beeped, radios came on, headlights flashed, sparks flew from their dashboards and engines turned themselves on and off. Soldiers who were sitting in or standing near their vehicles were thrown into a panic. They ran away from their crazed machines.

'What *is* going on?' Professor Stevens murmured.

She looked upward and soon got her answer.

Darkness covered the entire site as the shadow of a gigantic spaceship fell across it. All ground personnel froze in their tracks and stared up with open mouths. The whirring noise and the blinding lights had been coming from the spaceship.

Was it an invasion?

'Unbelievable!' said Professor Stevens.

'I'm going!' yelled one of the soldiers.

'Run!' shouted another.

Dropping their weapons and abandoning their vehicles, the Army personnel took to their heels and fled. Professor Stevens, the only person brave enough to stay, pulled something from her pocket.

It was a video camera. She was a true scientist and knew that her first duty was to record the strange phenomenon. Professor Stevens stood her ground, therefore, and saw everything.

The spaceship lowered itself gently on to the crater

like a giant bird settling on its nest. There was a distant sound of doors being hydraulically opened and shut then the craft rose slowly into the air. Once clear of the mountains, it emitted a roar of power and streaked off across the sky.

'That was incredible!' decided Professor Stevens.

She turned her camera from the sky back to the crater.

Unaware of her, a soldier in a radiation suit stepped out from behind a nearby rock. He removed his mask and let out an evil chuckle.

'What a bunch of suckers!'

Cliff Dagger was a big, brawny man with piggy eyes set in a craggy face. A black cap was pulled down low and covered part of his ugly features. He pulled out a small remote-control device and pressed its buttons.

Vehicles all around him came to life, honking their horns or flashing their lights. Dagger grinned. He had fooled the Army with his little device. The plan had worked perfectly.

Professor Stevens, meanwhile, had walked cautiously towards the edge of the crater. The radiation level had gone down now and it was safe to approach. She understood why. Though the plants were still growing around the crater, there was no sign of the meteor.

It had been taken away by the spaceship.

'Oh, no!' she exclaimed. 'It's gone!'

Dagger scowled as he noticed her for the first time. He moved towards her with menace in his voice.

'You've seen *way* too much, Mister!'

He grabbed Professor Stevens with rough hands then pulled off her radiation mask. Dagger was taken completely by surprise. Expecting to see a man, he was instead looking at an attractive young woman.

'It's not Mister,' she confirmed. 'It's Miss.'

Taking advantage of his astonishment, she kicked him hard on the shin. He let go of her to clutch at his leg and she raced off with her video camera as fast as she could.

'Come back!' he howled, hopping on one leg.

'No, thanks!' she called.

'We'll get you!'

Professor Stevens reached a jeep and dived straight into it. Its engine started and she vanished in a cloud of dust. She had got a vital piece of film but somebody was determined to take it from her.

Cliff Dagger. The enforcer of the VENOM group.

Limping towards a boulder, he went behind it and got into his assault vehicle, Jackhammer. It had front hood slides over the windshield for protection and reciprocating cannons behind the front grille. Its pop-up rear turret fired twin cannons rapid-fire with a 360 degree swivel. Jackhammer was something special.

As he gunned the engine to go after his prey, he reached for a microphone then flicked a switch.

'Rax!'

'Yeah?' said a low voice.

'You got company coming.'

Sly Rax was on his Piranha some distance away. A

cunning warrior and a weapons expert, Rax was another vital member of the VENOM team. His vehicle, Piranha, was a motorcycle with sidecar submarine. It had recessed machine guns in the front cowling and could also release ground torpedoes. Machine gun turrets were forward mounted on the sidecar. Underwater they could fire electric spears.

Rax was riding on his favourite murder weapon.

'Get out the welcome mat!' suggested Dagger.

'No sweat,' replied his colleague into the microphone. 'You can clean up when the party's over.'

He goaded the Piranha into top speed and set off in pursuit of the jeep that was now haring across the open desert. Dagger was not far behind him. VENOM was running down Professor Stevens.

When she realised that she was being followed, the scientist pressed her foot down hard on the accelerator to get every last ounce of speed out of the jeep. But she soon saw that she simply did not have the pace to outrun them.

Piranha and Jackhammer got steadily closer.

'I must save the film,' she resolved.

Driving with one hand, she used the other to remove the video cassette from the camera and slip it into her pocket. She then glanced in her rear-view mirror and gulped.

'Oh dear!'

They were well within firing range now.

'This ought to slow you down,' sneered Rax, pressing a button. 'Launching ground torpedoes!'

The torpedoes shot away barely clearing the ground and headed straight at the jeep. Professor Stevens saw them coming. A second before impact, she swung the driving wheel over so that her vehicle made a sudden lurch to the right.

Zigzagging viciously past her, the torpedoes exploded against a rock face and caused a small avalanche. Sly Rax had to dodge the boulders as they came tumbling towards him.

'You won't get away!' he roared.

'Leave it to me!' said Dagger into his microphone as he reached for a button. 'Fire cannons!'

The cannons barked furiously but they were off target. Instead of hitting the jeep, the shells fell short and exploded with a loud bang. Small craters were opened up and Rax had to swerve wildly to save himself from driving into them.

'Hey! Watch it, Dagger!' complained Rax.

'You should've hit her with the torpedoes.'

'Save those cannons till you're closer.'

The jeep had now reached the edge of the desert and joined a proper tarmac road. It enabled Professor Stevens to go faster and to enjoy the feeling that she might, after all, get away safely.

The two members of the VENOM team had other ideas.

'Stop her before she gets to the city!' ordered Dagger.

'No problem,' replied Rax.

'Shoot her tyres from under her.'

'Just for starters.'

Sly Rax smirked and urged the Piranha on. He began to eat up the distance between himself and the fleeing jeep. This time he would make no mistake. He would get close enough to be certain of a direct hit.

'What are you waiting for, Rax?' demanded Dagger.

'That bend up ahead.'

'Why?'

'You'll see!'

A precipice was just ahead of them and the road curved sharply away from it. Rax bided his time. As the jeep was just about to go into the bend, he jabbed a finger down on a button.

'Firing machine guns!'

Piranha's machine guns spat angrily and a stream of bullets ripped into the rear tyres of the jeep, causing them to blow out. Professor Stevens had no chance.

The vehicle went into an uncontrollable spin and left the road at the crown of the bend. After bouncing off a few rocks, it went over the edge of the precipice and plummeted all the way down to the dark water below.

It hit the lake with vicious impact and disappeared.

Dagger and Rax watched from the lip of the precipice.

'Nobody could survive that crash,' said Dagger.

'Too bad!' Rax commented. 'She was a good driver.'

'But not a good *diver*.'

They exchanged a grim laugh and walked off.

VENOM had triumphed again.

TWO

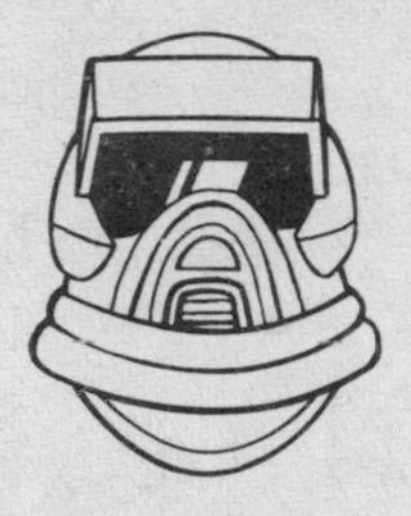

The mansion was an imposing sight. Standing in its own extensive grounds, it was a huge building with gracious proportions and lots of character. Expensive cars were parked in the garage. Gardeners were busy mowing the vast lawns. The swimming pool was glistening in the afternoon sun.

Evidently, the house was owned by a millionaire.

Matt Trakker. Leader and tactician of MASK.

He was in his study, pacing up and down. It was a large, well-appointed room that had been tastefully decorated. Bookshelves lined one whole wall and several trophies were standing between the rows of books. Framed certificates of merit were hanging everywhere.

A map of the world occupied another wall. There was also an ornate antique desk with a high-backed leather chair behind it. Directly behind the desk itself was a large mirror that reflected the light and made the room seem even bigger than it was.

Tall, powerfully built and impeccably dressed in a white suit, Matt Trakker paused to arrange some flowers in a vase. He looked up as he saw something. Lying on a leather couch with a blanket over her, was a lovely young woman. Her eyes were shut and there was a bandage around her forehead.

Matt Trakker crossed to her as she stirred.

'Hello, Professor Stevens,' he said with a kind smile.

'Oh,' she muttered, blinking her eyes.

'Feeling better?'

'Where am I?'

'In my home, Professor Stevens.'

'How do you know my name?' she wondered.

'It's printed on your radiation suit,' he pointed out.

She glanced down at the name stitched above the breast pocket. Her head slowly began to clear and she recalled what had happened.

'I was driving a jeep.'

'It went over a precipice.'

'Last thing I remember was the jeep spinning like crazy.'

'You must have been thrown clear,' he explained. 'My men found you behind a rock near the cliff edge.'

'I was chased across the desert. They fired at me.'

'You're safe now,' he assured her, easing her back

on the couch as she tried to sit up. 'Nobody will hurt you here.'

'Who are you?' she asked.

'I'm Matt Trakker.'

'Matt Trakker!' she repeated. 'I've *heard* of you.'

'Have you?' he said, breaking off one of the flowers in the vase to insert it in his buttonhole. 'I hope the reports were good.'

'Better than good!'

'That's nice to hear, Professor.'

'You're supposed to help people in trouble.'

'You could put it that way.'

'Boy!' she exclaimed. 'Could I use some help now.'

'So could a lot of people, Professor Stevens, but I'm not able to help them all, I'm afraid. There just isn't the time.'

'Then who *do* you help, Mr Trakker?'

'My interest lies in rather unusual situations.'

'Unusual?'

'Matters of life and death,' he said. 'My organisation is committed to fight on the side of good against evil. We only take on cases of serious crime.'

'They don't come any more serious than this,' she promised, reaching into her pocket for the video cassette. 'Maybe you'd better take a look at this film.'

'Why?'

'Because then you'll understand what it's all about,' added Professor Stevens, handing the cassette to him. 'A question of life and death for millions of people!'

Matt Trakker's interest quickened at once.

The Games Room was in another part of the mansion. It was a children's paradise and was filled with all kinds of things. There were arcade-style video games, a pool table, a table-tennis table, a punchball, an elaborate layout for electric trains, model aeroplanes, toys galore and a whole variety of electronic gizmos.

It had everything a child needs.

Except other children.

Scott Trakker, the adopted son of Matt, was an alert and lively young boy with a taste for mischief. He was playing table tennis with Thingamebob, the short and rather comical-looking robot with the domed head and round, staring eyes.

He called his friend T-Bob. Scott liked playing against him because he always beat the robot. As the boy slammed a backhand shot across the table, it screamed off the other side and hit the floor.

'Awright!' shouted Scott, happily. 'I won again!'

'I hate this game,' moaned T-Bob. 'I quit.'

He threw down his bat in disgust but used far too much force. It rebounded off the table and gave him a smack in the face.

Scott went off into peals of laughter.

'It's not funny,' complained T-Bob in his piping voice. 'I'm just not programmed to beat you at ping-pong.'

'No, *I'm* programmed to beat *you*.'

'I want to play something else.'

'Okay, T-Bob,' said Scott. 'Let's play spies and see what Dad's doing. Go to motorscooter mode!'

The robot obeyed at once and converted himself into

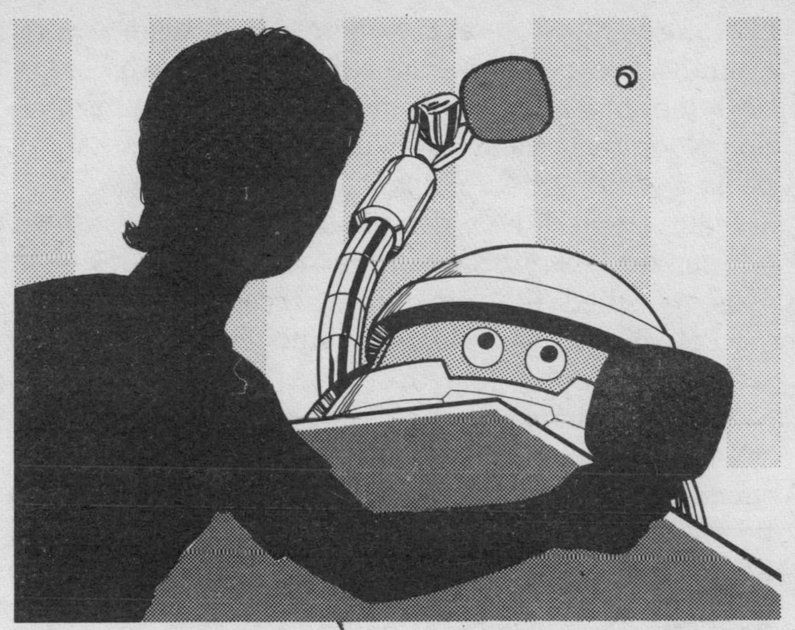

a small scooter. Jumping on to the seat, Scott twisted the control on the handlebars and they raced out of the room in a flash.

They were in search of fun.

Matt Trakker sat in front of a modular multi-buttoned desk in his Observation Room. Facing him was the reverse side of the two-way mirror that hung behind the antique desk in his study. It was thus possible for him to look through and see Professor Stevens lying on the leather couch. He was touched by her plight and hoped that he would be able to help her.

The room was dominated by the computer and its assorted monitoring and analysing devices. Rapidly blinking lights were everywhere. There were several numerical readouts on the console. While the study next door had an old-fashioned comfort, the Observation Room was gleaming with metallic newness and packed with high technology.

Matt watched the video film on a large screen.

'I see what the Professor means!' he sighed.

He watched the spaceship descend to carry the meteor away, then Dagger's sinister face filled the screen in hideous close-up.

'Hold it right there,' he ordered.

The monitor freeze-framed Dagger's face. Then there was a low humming sound as the complex personal computer rose out of the surface of the desk. Matt wanted a detailed check.

'Analysis!' he ordered.

As readouts of the objects appeared on the screen, the computer analysed in a flat, impersonal, female voice.

'UFO: terrestrial in origin.

METEOR: potentially lethal in enemy hands.

Confirmation of enemy: VENOM.

Recommended course of action: assemble MASK.'

Matt Trakker was so involved in what he was doing that he did not notice the door being inched open behind him. Scott and T-Bob were eavesdropping. They wanted to be in on the action.

'Scan on Professor Stevens,' said Matt.

The computer revealed its findings in the same dull voice.

'All scans normal. Beta probe, cardiogram, polygraph cleared.

Recommended course of action: plenty of rest.'

Matt flicked a switch to put his voice through.

'All right, Professor Stevens,' he said. 'Consider me handling the situation. In the meantime, just stay here and rest.'

The scientist could not see through her side of the mirror and she wondered where his voice came from. She looked all round the room but could spot no speakers.

'Please hurry, Mr Trakker,' she urged. 'The radioactive power in that meteor is the key to my new life-saving technique. In my hands, it could be a boon to mankind. But the wrong people could use it for destruction!'

'Not if I can help it, Professor!' he warned.

Scott turned eagerly to T-Bob who had converted back now.

'We got us a mission, T-Bob!'

Matt Trakker whirled around in his chair.

'Scott!' he called, sharply. 'Get in here!'

They had been caught in the act and they knew it. Shamefaced and embarrassed, Scott and T-Bob emerged from behind the door and came into the room. They stood in front of Matt and looked down at the floor. Both felt the discomfort.

'I hope you weren't eavesdropping,' said Matt.

T-Bob looked up and nodded but Scott immediately tried to deny the charge by shaking his head vigorously. The boy switched on a big, phoney smile.

'Who? Me?' he asked. 'No, sir! Can I go now?'

Matt guessed the truth and was tolerant.

'You can go,' he agreed, 'but I want you to keep Professor Stevens company. I've got something else to do. Understand?'

'Roger, Dad!' replied Scott.

'Do *you* understand, T-Bob?' asked Matt.

'Yes, sir!'

Without waiting to be asked, the robot changed himself into a motorscooter again and carried his passenger out of the room. As they went through the door, Scott closed it firmly behind them.

Matt smiled then swung round to face the computer again. The small video camera set into it now swivelled around to focus on him.

'Give me the data on the best agents for this mission.'

The screen flashed with static and then showed a face along with computer graphics of a specialist vehicle.

'Personnel collected,' announced the computer. 'Brad Turner, motorcyclist and helicopter pilot. Expert ratings in both. Vehicle code name: Condor.'

'Approved,' said Matt.

'Bruce Sato. Expert mechanical engineer and mechanical specialist. Vehicle code name: Rhino.'

'Approved.'

'Alex Sector. Computer and communication expert. Systems commander. Vehicle code name: Rhino.'

'Approved.'

'Hondo MacLean. Weapon specialist and tactical strategist. Vehicle code name: Firecracker.'

'Approved.'

'Dusty Hayes. Auto and marine stunt driver. Vehicle code name: Gator.'

'Approved.'

'Buddie Hawkes. Master of disguise, impersonations and intelligence gathering. Vehicle code name: Firecracker.'

'Approved,' said Matt.

They were without doubt his finest agents.

Brad Turner. Bruce Sato. Alex Sector. Hondo MacLean. Dusty Hayes. Buddy Hawkes. Outstanding men with outstanding talents.

'Assemble Mobile Armoured Strike Kommand!'

As he gave the order, Matt Trakker pressed a button on his watch. The word MASK flashed on the liquid-crystal display.

The wristwatch sent its signal to the six agents who had been chosen.

Brad Turner was playing guitar in a small rock band at a banquet. When he saw his watch blinking away, he hurriedly unstrapped his instrument and walked off the stage. He ignored the complaints of his fellow-musicians and rushed away.

MASK business was paramount. Everything else came second.

The other five agents responded in the same prompt way.

Bruce Sato, a toy designer, was piecing together a remote-control model aircraft when the call came. He put his work aside at once and ran out of the room at speed.

The affable Dusty Hayes was serving a customer in his Pizza Parlour. He threw the dough high in the air then noticed his watch flashing its signal. Dusty strode off and let the dough land with a plop on the floor.

Alex Sector also left a bemused customer behind him. He ran a pet shop that specialised in exotic snakes and he was holding a large boa constrictor. When the summons came, he simply handed the snake to a little old lady and barged out through the door. She was horrified as the boa constrictor coiled itself around her.

Hondo MacLean, a history teacher at a high school, was busy supervising an examination. His students were bent over their desks, scribbling hard with their pens. A watch flashed, a door slammed and they suddenly had no teacher in the room.

Buddie Hawkes caused equal consternation at the Boulder Hill Gas Station where he worked. He was just about to serve a man with petrol when the signal came. Without a word of explanation, he simply turned around and trotted quickly away.

MASK took priority over everything.

The men knew that they would only be summoned if they were needed for a very special mission and that is why they rushed to obey the command.

Matt Trakker wanted them at once.

It was a dire emergency.

THREE

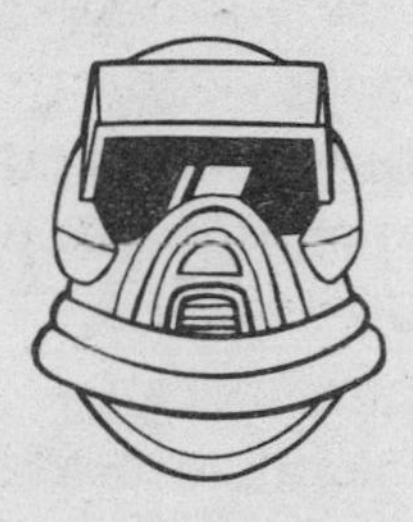

Matt Trakker crossed swiftly to the far wall of the Observation Room. It was covered with banks of complicated equipment. When he pressed a button, the whole wall slid away with an electronic hum. Matt stepped through into a secret passage and the wall automatically slid back into position behind him.

Waiting nearby on a tube-like track was his bullet shuttle, a streamlined rocket car that was capable of carrying several people. He got inside and gave the command.

'MASK headquarters. Rocket mode.'

The shuttle hurtled down the tube at supersonic speed.

There was no time to waste.

Back in the Observation Room, the door opened slowly and a boy's head came around it. Scott Trakker relaxed when he saw that the place was empty. He led T-Bob into the room and crossed to the sliding wall.

'MASK is going to need us if they're up against VENOM.'

'Er, Scott,' reminded T-Bob, nervously. 'Didn't Matt tell us to stay here and keep Professor Stevens company?'

'You heard the computer,' said Scott, airily. 'Professor Stevens needs rest, not company. We'd only be in the way.'

'That's nothing new.'

'Besides, MASK wants our help.'

'Nobody's asked for it,' argued the robot.

'That makes no difference,' replied Scott, pressing the button so that the wall slid away. 'Come on, T-Bob.'

'I still think we could be making a mistake.'

'You're not *scared*, are you?' teased the boy.

'Not scared,' admitted T-Bob. 'Just terrified.'

'Go to motorscooter mode!' ordered Scott.

The robot converted immediately and the boy jumped on.

'Look out, VENOM!' he warned. 'Here we come!'

They roared off down the tube at maximum speed.

The main laboratory at VENOM headquarters was a huge room filled with computers, gleaming machinery and the very latest technological wonders.

Standing on a metal table against a wall, was the meteor. It seemed to be throbbing with life and bathed the whole place with its blue-coloured energy.

A steel shutter lifted in the wall to reveal a dozen large plant-pots containing nothing but bare earth. Once exposed to the power of the meteor, however, the earth immediately put forth shoots that grew and blossomed within seconds.

'Excellent!' remarked a deep voice.

Miles Mayhem, head of VENOM, observed the whole process from behind a protective wall of glass. A big, solid man with bushy eyebrows and an even bushier moustache, Mayhem wore the uniform of a

Supreme Commander. There was an air of undeniable authority about him.

Standing beside him were two of his henchmen, Cliff Dagger and Sly Rax. They watched as their leader manipulated a joystick.

'Now to see if my theory is correct.'

As Mayhem operated the controls, a robot arm wheeled into place above the meteor and fired a pin-point laser straight into the rock. There was an explosion of rainbow colours and crackling waves of energy burst from the meteor. When the lightshow subsided, the meteor was split into three separate parts.

The colour of the pulsating energy had now turned from blue to a glowing red. It was red for danger.

The plants turned red as well and shrivelled instant-

ly. One by one, the pots exploded with astounding force and the fragments went everywhere. It was a vivid demonstration of the meteor's power.

Miles Mayhem rubbed his hands together with glee.

'Fantastic!' he shouted. 'The destructive capacity of those pieces is just as I suspected. We're going to be *rich*!'

'Are we?' said Sly Rax.

'Here is a list of countries that would love to buy the greatest weapon on Earth,' said Mayhem, giving Rax a slip of paper. 'Tell them the bidding starts at fifty million dollars for one piece.'

'One piece of what?' asked Dagger.

'That!' hissed Mayhem, pointing to the meteor. 'The Deathstone!'

The three pieces of the meteor sat on the table and radiated a red aura of destruction. Smoking debris lay all around it.

The Deathstone. It was the perfect name.

From the front, the Boulder Hill Gas Station looked like any other modern installation of its kind and it carried out its normal business from day to day. But it provided much more than a service to passing motorists. It was a major defence mechanism.

Beneath the garage was MASK headquarters.

Various weapon systems had been concealed at ground level. The gas pumps supplied petrol but they could also fire freeze rays and they swivelled to give a wide firing range. Inside the shop was a cannon that fired an anti-gravity beam. Above the shop was a landing pad for a helicopter.

Boulder Hill itself loomed up behind the station. Set into the rock and cunningly hidden from view was a turret that swivelled to fire lasers. The final deadly weapon was a massive boulder that seemed to be part of the hill. It could be released to crash down on an enemy below and had proven its worth more than once.

Located deep underground in MASK headquarters, the Briefing Room had the appearance of a war room. Banks of computers stood everywhere and lights flashed permanently. One wall was occupied by an electronic map of the world. There was a great sense of order and purpose about the entire place.

Matt Trakker was no longer the relaxed and casual millionaire who had been chatting to Professor Stevens in his study. Dressed in his dark uniform with its special pouches and shoulder harness, he looked an impressive figure.

All the members of his team were there. Each man wore his combat outfit but not his mask. They listened carefully as Matt briefed them and showed them the video film of the meteor.

'So now you know everything I do,' he said. 'As always, secrecy is of the highest priority.'

'Where is the meteor now?' asked Hondo MacLean.

'Patch into the radiation tracking satellite, Alex,' ordered Matt. 'We need a fix on that thing.'

'Give me a few seconds,' answered Alex Sector.

Alex Sector, a tall man with a distinctive bald head and full beard, sat in front of a control panel and flicked various switches. A red blip soon began to flash on the electronic wall map. Alex indicated the area with a long finger.

'There she is,' he announced. 'Nevada.'

'That's the meteor all right,' agreed Matt. 'Let's move it!'

He led the way on to a rapidly-moving escalator that took them up to a thick metal door. On a command from Matt, the door swung open to give access to a semi-circular room with an array of masks hanging from the smooth walls. Electronic equipment was fixed into the ceiling high above. There was a subdued energy about the whole place.

On the floor were pre-marked spaces, arranged in a full circle like the designated seats of King Arthur's Round Table. As the men entered the room, they took up their allotted places and formed a circle that looked inwards.

The door of the Energiser Room closed behind them.

Matt Trakker put down his briefcase before taking up his own position in the circle. He looked around the faces of his colleagues to make sure that they were all ready then gave the order.

'Stand by for mask charging!'

A vitally important ritual now took place.

There was a constant electronic whine. From above and behind each man, long armature arms descended

to lift the various masks from the walls. The metal arms held the respective masks over each man so that he could reach up and touch it. The men carefully angled the masks away from their bodies.

'Mask charging – now!' commanded Matt.

A laser beam suddenly appeared from the ceiling and split into a dazzling starburst pattern that threw frantic shadows on the walls. Each ray of the laser zapped directly to one of the masks to energise it. The men were bathed in a bright, warm glow.

Every one of them had his specific headgear.

Matt Trakker stood below Spectrum, a mask that gave him free-fall abilities and which could also emit shrill noises to unsettle a foe. It was the mask he always used when he travelled in Thunder Hawk.

Brad Turner, the rock musician, was positioned beneath Hocus Pocus, a mask that could project holographic images which could be used to deceive and baffle an enemy.

Bruce Sato's mask was called Lifter because it could fire an anti-gravity beam that enabled him to lift and move heavy objects.

Alex Sector, the oldest man in the team, would soon be wearing Jackrabbit, a high-powered mask that allowed him rocket flight and thus the ability to take off like a jackrabbit.

The fearless Hondo MacLean stood below Blaster, a mask that contained an Internal Guidance System for his shoulder-launched lasers and made him a particularly dangerous warrior.

BOULDER HILL
GAS

The mask belonging to Dusty Hayes, the pizza cook, was named Backlash because it could fire shock waves on land or underwater.

Buddie Hawkes, the master of disguise, was holding Penetrator, a mask which enabled both its user and his vehicle to move through solid objects.

Seven brave men.

Seven special masks.

One mission: to thwart VENOM.

A fierce electronic buzz was heard and then the entire floor began to rise. The men were able to take the masks from the arms that held them and to put them on.

'To the transports!' shouted Matt Trakker.

The garage which stood at the rear of the Boulder Hill Gas Station contained a few cars awaiting repair. Responding to a signal, the back wall opened up to admit several pairs of mechanical arms. The cars were lifted up and taken out of the garage to be stored on special metal racks.

The MASK vehicles now came into view.

Rising dramatically out of the floor on hydraulic lifts, the vehicles were glinting in the lights and ready for action. Matt and his men arrived on their elevated platform and then ran to get into their respective vehicles. The door of the garage lifted and the vehicles tore out at speed.

Matt Trakker set the pace in Thunder Hawk.

Bruce Sato and Alex Sector followed him in Rhino.

Next came Brad Turner on Condor.

Dusty Hayes zipped after him in Gator.

Firecracker, the pickup truck, brought up the rear.

Hondo MacLean and Buddie Hawkes were inside the last vehicle as it powered its way along the road. What they did not know was that they had stowaways. Hidden beneath a tarpaulin in the rear of the truck were two familiar figures.

They peeped out to see what was going on.

'Isn't this exciting?' said Scott Trakker.

'No,' replied T-Bob, anxiously. 'Something tells me I'd rather be playing ping-pong.'

'We need some real action,' asserted Scott, boldly. 'And that's what we're going to get!'

He was right.

FOUR

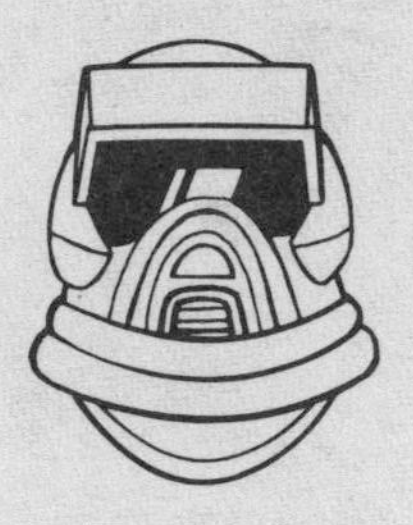

The Mobile Armoured Strike Kommand rolled across the Nevada desert.

Sitting in Rhino, the thoughtful Bruce Sato studied the photo of the spaceship that had been seen by Professor Stevens. There was something odd about the craft. He tried to work out what it was.

Bruce Sato was Matt Trakker's closest friend. He had a keen intelligence, a dry wit and – with his Oriental background – he was a true philosopher.

Rhino was a superb war machine.

A big, heavy truck, it had a front grille that could convert to a power ram bumper and diesel smokestacks that became 180 degree cannon. It could put up a rear smokescreen and had a Multi-Warhead

Missile launcher in its sleeper cab. Rhino was also fitted with radar that had mobile command centre capabilities and with ejection seats for a real emergency. The rear of the truck converted into an all-terrain vehicle (ATV) with front-mounted cannons.

Inside the steel monster was a sharp mind.

It belonged to Bruce Sato.

He flicked a switch and spoke into the microphone.

'Matt, this is Bruce.'

'I hear you,' replied Matt from inside Thunder Hawk.

'Regarding the spacecraft . . .'

'Yeah?'

'If a fish flies, look not for a fish but a bird inside.'

Buddie Hawkes heard the message inside Firecracker.

'There he goes again, Matt!' he said with a sigh. 'Not making any sense. Why can't Bruce speak in plain English?'

'He did, Buddie,' returned Matt over the microphone.

'You could have fooled me!'

'What Bruce means is this,' explained Matt. 'VENOM obviously used their helicopter inside a phoney UFO shell.'

'There was no real spaceship, then?' asked Buddy.

'No. Just Miles Mayhem up to his old tricks.'

The vehicles sped on across the barren landscape.

VENOM's cement bunker was a large, low structure in a desert area. At first sight, nothing appeared to be standing anywhere near it. Then six hefty men came out of the bunker to pull back a huge sand-coloured camouflage blanket. VENOM vehicles were revealed. As well as Piranha and Jackhammer, there were three large trucks.

And the spaceship.

Miles Mayhem, Sly Rax and Cliff Dagger emerged from the bunker to watch their thugs at work. The men carefully removed the sheet-metal exterior of the spaceship. Underneath the false panels was Switchblade, the VENOM helicopter-jet.

Mayhem grinned with pleasure then snarled an order.

'Let's move it! We have some deliveries to make!'

The thugs ran over to the three trucks. Two men leapt into each one and the vehicles drove off in different directions. Mayhem turned to his henchmen.

'Stay close to those trucks. I'll observe from the air in case anyone tries to get in our way.'

'Like MASK!' sneered Rax.

'Who else?' added Mayhem.

'It's time we finished them for good,' argued Rax.

'We will,' promised his leader. 'Don't worry. We will.'

Sly Rax mounted Piranha and pulled on his mask. It was called Stiletto because it fired stiletto-type darts

and underwater harpoons. Rax drove off after one of the MASK trucks.

Cliff Dagger sat in Jackhammer as it zoomed off after another of the MASK trucks. His repulsive face was now hidden beneath Torch, a mask which turns into a lethal flame-thrower.

Miles Mayhem stepped into Switchblade and fitted his own Viper mask that could spit corrosive poison. As the machine lifted off, he thought about his arch-enemy and gave a dark cackle.

'We'll get you, Trakker!' he vowed. 'Once and for all!'

VENOM – the Vicious Evil Network Of Mayhem – had spoken.

Inside Thunder Hawk, Matt Trakker was making use of the mini-tracking screen that was in his briefcase. He watched the three red dots moving in different directions and realised what must have happened.

He reached for his microphone to give an order.

'Trident manoeuvre! The meteor must have been broken up. Split into three groups and follow!'

The MASK vehicles obeyed at once.

High above the desert, Switchblade caught its first glimpse of the enemy. Mayhem brought the machine down so that he could take a closer look at what was going on. He saw his three trucks being chased separately by MASK vehicles.

'So they figured out I split the meteor!' he said, punching his thigh with a fist. 'They'll wish they never interfered.' He snarled to his machine. 'Switchblade – *switch*!'

The helicopter immediately turned into a jet aircraft. Its weapon systems were formidable. It could fire two "stinger" rockets and it had recessed nose cannons as well as skid cannons.

It was also extremely fast.

Alex Sector was the first to spot the jet on his radar. He grasped the microphone to raise the alarm.

'Attention all vehicles!'

'We hear you loud and clear,' said Matt.

'Unidentified aircraft coming in at full speed. Watch your backs, everybody!'

'Thanks for the warning, Alex.'

'Take evasive action, Matt.'

'I'll do better than that.'

Matt Trakker was screaming along a dirt track in his vehicle. He made sure that his safety harness was locked firmly in position before he gave the command.

'Thunder Hawk – jet mode.'

The change was instantaneous.

Both doors swung outwards and upwards to form gull wings. The chassis of the car changed shape and jet engines supplied a great surge of power. Thunder Hawk accelerated then lifted off and began to explore the sky.

Matt held on as he was thrown backwards by the take-off.

His aircraft was a flying weapon. Its wings could fire lasers both in the air and on the ground. It could drop

magnetic bombs which attached themselves to a target and permitted remote-control detonation. Thunder Hawk also carried additional bombs for aerial surveillance, sonic disruption and melting capabilities.

It was the spearhead of the MASK attack.

'Now, then,' said Matt. 'Where's this aircraft?'

He got an answer to his question at once.

Switchblade swooped down until it got Condor in its sights then it fired its wing cannons. The ground around Brad Turner was sprayed with bullets as the aircraft flew past. He fought to control his motorcycle as it swerved madly to and fro.

'I knew it!' he yelled. 'I just knew it!'

Firecracker was driving close behind and Hondo MacLean could see the problems that his friend was having.

'Take it easy there, Brad!' he advised.

'I'm gonna play this gig from the air, Hondo.'

'Good idea!'

'Condor!' ordered Brad. 'Fly!'

The motorcycle converted at once to a helicopter and took to the sky. As well as a nose cannon that fired an anti-matter ray, Brad Turner now had two belly cannons at his disposal. Being airborne made him feel less like a target.

He was now in a position to strike back.

Firecracker, meanwhile, rumbled along at speed with Hondo MacLean and Buddie Hawkes seated in its cab. One moment they were alone in the desert, the next moment they had company.

A VENOM vehicle was on their tail.

Jackhammer had been lurking behind some thick, scrubby underbrush. As Firecracker went past, the machine set off in pursuit. Wearing his mask, Cliff Dagger appeared in the gun turret and began firing at the pickup truck.

Hondo MacLean put out a distress signal at once.

'Mayday! Mayday! We need some back-up here!'

Instead of getting help, however, Firecracker had to suffer an additional threat. Switchblade had banked in the air and turned to come straight back at the truck.

'Mayday!' repeated Hondo into his microphone. 'Mayday! Mayday!'

'Sounds like trouble,' noted Matt Trakker.

Firecracker was threatened from the ground and from the air.

'Let's see you outrun this one!' challenged Miles Mayhem, high up in Switchblade. 'Locking missile on pickup truck!'

The jet fired a stinger missile at Firecracker.

It was right on target.

Brad Turner flew in on Condor from another angle.

'Firing Hocus Pocus mask!'

The missile streaked down towards the pickup truck at the very moment that a multi-coloured beam shone out of Brad's mask. The beam created a three-dimensional replica of Firecracker that hovered in mid-air just behind the missile.

It turned itself around and chased after the holographic projection. The projection in turn aimed itself

at Switchblade. Even Miles Mayhem was fooled by it. As he saw a truck hurtling through space at him, he flinched away.

'Oh, no!' he cried.

But the projection slowly disintegrated into nothingness. The missile now had no target and so it headed straight at Switchblade. With great aerial skill, the jet pulled up sharply so that the missile shot harmlessly past it to explode some distance away.

Mayhem was livid.

'How did he *do* that to me. It's not fair!'

Hondo and Buddie were very grateful to their colleague.

'Thanks a lot, Brad,' said Hondo.

'We'll do the same for you one day,' promised Buddie.

'My pleasure,' replied Brad.

For two of the passengers, however, Firecracker's escape had been far too close for comfort. Scott Trakker and T-Bob peeped out from beneath their tarpaulin in the rear of the truck.

'Wow!' exclaimed the boy.

'Pulsating ping-pong balls!' wailed the robot.

'That hologram mask is really something!'

'Just get me out of here!' pleaded T-Bob.

'Yes,' agreed Scott. 'Maybe it wasn't such a good idea to stow away on this mission. The action is a little *too* hot.'

'You can say that again!'

T-Bob hid under the tarpaulin as more danger threatened.

It was Piranha's turn to attack Firecracker. Emerging from its hiding place in the brush, it headed straight for the truck. Sly Rax gave the order into his microphone.

'Launching ground torpedo!'

Rax pressed a button on his handlebars and a torpedo shot away on its lethal journey towards Firecracker. At the same time, Rhino swung in to tackle the VENOM machine.

'Try this one for size!' said Bruce Sato. 'Lifter beam – on!'

A blast of energy fired from his mask and lifted

VENOM

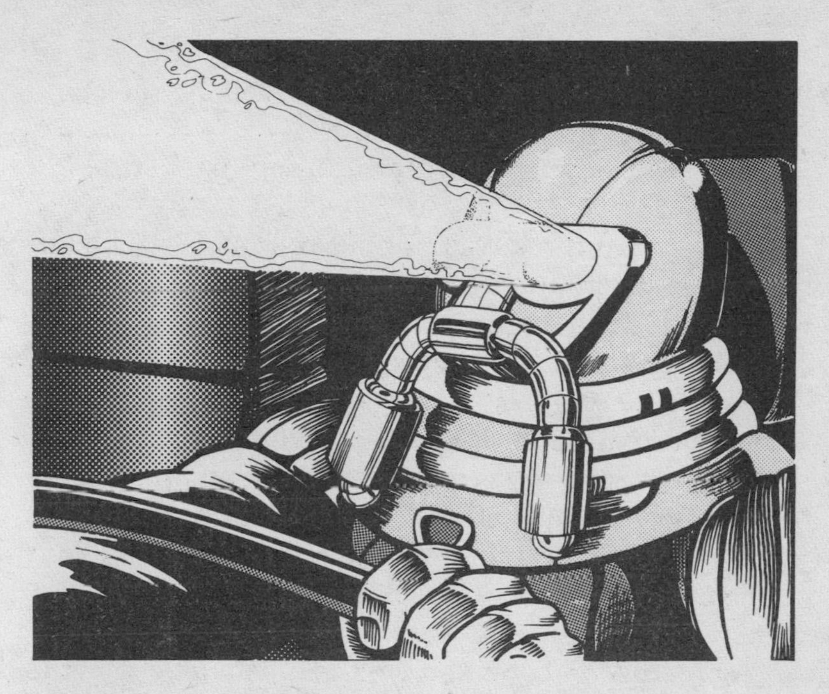

Piranha right off the ground. As the beam swept across the torpedo, it threw the missile off its trajectory and into the air a split-second before it would have exploded against Firecracker.

'Thanks, Bruce!' called Hondo.

'Our second rescue today,' observed Buddie.

'I haven't done with this jerk yet,' said Bruce.

The laser beam lifted Piranha even higher and turned it over. Rax was left hanging helplessly from the handlebars. The torpedo, meanwhile, was flying crazily around in the sky. It aimed itself at Rax and swished in on its new target.

'Get away!' he yelled. 'Not *me*!'

He opened his legs wide and the torpedo flashed between them, sending both Rax and his machine cartwheeling through the sky.

Bruce Sato laughed then turned back to Fire-cracker.

The pickup truck was not out of trouble. Jackhammer was still in pursuit, firing a stream of bullets at it. Hondo decided to return the compliment.

'Launch shredder!' he ordered.

The spare tyre – complete with murderous blades – was ejected back towards Jackhammer but the VENOM machine was ready for it. Dagger brought the front hood sliding up to form an armoured barrier over his windshield and the rotating tyre banged off it and rolled away.

Another menace now appeared.

A big truck pulled out from the brush directly in the path of Firecracker. Hondo MacLean was too busy looking in his wing mirrors to notice it at first. Bruce Sato shouted a warning from Rhino.

'Hondo! Look out!'

'Ooooh!' yelled Hondo when he saw the truck ahead.

He pulled the steering wheel hard to the left and barely avoided a collision with Rhino. The truck was now travelling on only two tyres as it screeched on. It had managed to miss crashing into the VENOM truck but there had been one casualty.

Scott Trakker had been thrown out of Fire-cracker.

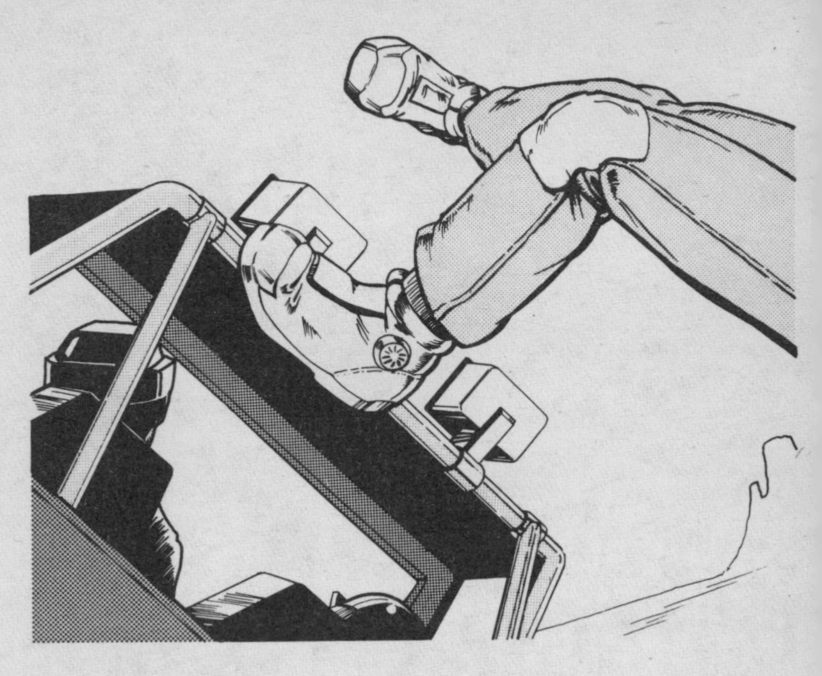

T-Bob leaned over the edge and cried out after his friend.

'Scott! Scott!'

It seemed as if he had lost the boy for good.

FIVE

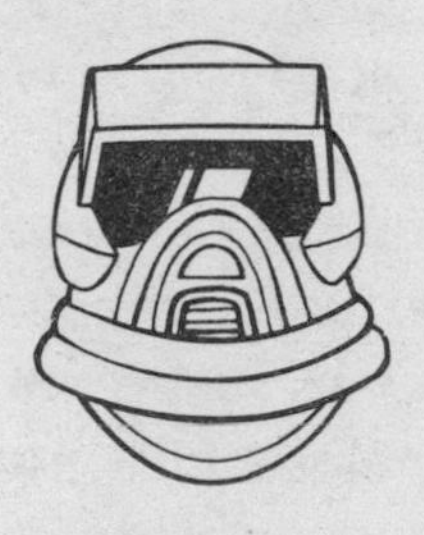

But Scott Trakker had not been killed by the fall. When he was hurled out of the back of the truck, he had been lucky enough to land on some soft shrubs. The boy was only slightly dazed. He had made a miraculous escape.

When he looked up, however, he saw that the danger was by no means over. Jackhammer was now racing straight at him with the obvious intention of running him down.

There was nowhere to run and nowhere to hide.

'Help!' he yelled. 'Help! Help!'

Gator came zooming out of the desert from behind Rhino and aimed itself at Jackhammer. Dusty Hayes, the brilliant stunt driver, was waving his hat as if he was riding a bucking bronco.

'Hang on, Scott!' he bellowed. 'Old Dusty's coming!'

'Help! Quick!'

'Yee-haa! Hit 'em with the ELECTRIC OUCH!'

Dusty fired the cannon that was mounted on Gator. It released a crackling ball of energy that shot towards Jackhammer and enveloped the pop-up turret in which Dagger was sitting. The whole turret was now fizzing with electricity.

Dagger jumped out of his seat as the current gave him a shock. When he grabbed the handle of his machine gun, however, he got an even bigger jolt. He screamed loudly as electricity crackled around him.

Jackhammer came to a juddering halt inches from Scott.

But as one danger vanished, yet another came on the scene.

Switchblade was making a third pass at the MASK vehicles with Thunder Hawk on its tail. The VENOM jet swooped low to drop a bomb and then pulled out of its dive to soar to the heavens once more.

Scott stared up in horror at the bomb.

It would blow him to pieces.

Then Hondo MacLean came sprinting towards him.

'Scott!' he shouted. 'Don't move!'

Hondo flung himself on top of the boy to protect him.

Brad Turner was hovering above the cacti in Condor. When he saw the bomb descending through the air, he took immediate action.

'Time for a little anti-matter.'

Condor released a blast of anti-matter beam from its nose cannon. It streaked towards the falling bomb.

Dusty Hayes did not want to be left out. He stood up in Gator and snapped a command to his Backlash mask.

'Firing torpedo!'

The torpedo and the anti-matter beam converged on the bomb from different angles. When all three met, there was a tremendous explosion that first expanded outward but was at once sucked back inward to form an implosion. The anti-matter beam had taken effect on the shrapnel and neutralised it.

The worst of the blast had been contained.

'That should hold 'em!' said Dusty, before driving off. 'We've got a job to finish.'

Brad Turner contacted Matt Trakker on his microphone.

'Matt! Your kid's here!'

'*Scott*?' he said in surprise.

'Yeah.'

'What on earth is he doing here?'

'He just missed being blown to smithereens.'

'I'm on my way!' decided Matt.

Thunder Hawk was busy chasing Switchblade across the blue sky when the message came through on the intercom. Matt was sorry to break off his pursuit but he had no choice.

The boy's safety came first.

Matt pulled back hard on the steering mechanism

and Thunder Hawk looped back on itself. Its pilot was now upside down as it rocketed back across the desert.

Scott, meanwhile, was still lying beneath Hondo MacLean.

He crawled out from beneath the inert body of the MASK agent. Hondo did not move at all. In trying to save Scott, he had taken the full force of the blast himself. Hondo had paid for his bravery.

T-Bob came rolling up as Scott looked down at the body.

'Hondo's hurt, T-Bob,' said the boy, almost crying.

'I can see that.'

'It's all *my* fault,' admitted Scott.

'What are we going to do?'

'Think.'

'Think?'

'About Professor Stevens.'

'Yes, she's very lovely,' said T-Bob.

'Think about what she *said*.'

'And what was that?' asked the robot.

'Professor Stevens said that the meteor can *save* lives.'

'Hondo is in need of a little saving right now.'

'Yes,' agreed the boy. 'He saved my life. It's time I returned the favour. Track 'em, T-Bob.'

'Okay,' said the robot, nervously. 'But I hope you know what you're doing, Scott.'

'Track 'em,' repeated his friend. 'Fast.'

They set off quickly across the desert.

Jackhammer had now recovered from the electric

current which had been fired at it by Gator. The VENOM machine limped away with Dagger clinging to its rear bumper. Rax followed on Piranha.

Mayhem's henchmen had had enough and were retreating.

Scott and T-Bob watched the vehicles leaving.

'Go to motorscooter mode!'

The robot obeyed and the boy mounted the scooter to chase after the fleeing VENOM agents. They had to help Hondo somehow.

Thunder Hawk came in to land nearby, sending up a cloud of dust as it did so. Matt Trakker ran across to his men. Dusty Hayes, Alex Sector and Bruce Sato were all kneeling beside the motionless body of Hondo MacLean.

'What happened?' asked Matt.

'Hondo's hurt bad,' explained Bruce.

'Where's Scott?'

'He's gone.'

'Which way?'

'That way,' answered Bruce, pointing a finger. 'After them.'

Matt Trakker looked in the direction indicated.

'VENOM . . .' he murmured.

One of the fleeing trucks hit a sharp rock as it trundled along and its front tyre started to go down. The driver pulled over and stopped. Scott and T-Bob stayed behind an outcrop of bushes until the man started to change the tyre. When his back was to them, they sneaked out from their hiding place and climbed into the rear of the vehicle.

T-Bob spoke in a low whisper.

'What are we doing here?'

'Searching for the meteor.'

'Why?'

'Because Hondo needs it. Professor Stevens said so.'

'But Professor Stevens has never met Hondo.'

'That doesn't matter.'

'Doesn't it?'

'The meteor is the key.'

T-Bob scratched his metallic head. It was all very confusing.

When the tyre had been changed, the truck continued its journey. The friends crouched down in the rear of the vehicle. They knew that they were taking a big risk but it was worth it.

Scott was determined to find the life-saving meteor.

In the battle-scarred area where the fight with VENOM had taken place, Alex Sector and Bruce Sato put Hondo MacLean on to a stretcher then strapped him gently into position. They lifted the stretcher and put it across the back seat of Thunder Hawk which had now converted back to a car.

Buddie Hawkes watched in consternation.

'Hondo doesn't look too good, man.'

'I know,' agreed Matt. 'That blast hit him hard.'

'Matt,' croaked Hondo, opening an eye. 'What's going on?'

'Take it easy,' advised the other.

'I feel bad.'

'We'll get you to a doctor as soon as we can.'

Matt got into Thunder Hawk and it started up. Hondo tried to force a smile as he spoke but he was in great pain.

'Don't worry about me. Just stop those meteor fragments from leaving the country. That's the important thing, Matt.'

'You're pretty important as well,' reminded Matt. 'That's why I'm taking you back. You need medical attention urgently.'

'What happened to Scott?' asked the patient.

'You saved his life.'

'Good.'

'You're very courageous, Hondo.'

'Thanks.'

'Scott will never forget what you did for him.'

'Where is he now?'

Matt Trakker heaved a sigh and shook his head sadly.

'I wish I knew, Hondo. I wish I knew.'

The VENOM truck reached an abandoned lakeside dock and came to a halt. Switchblade hovered for a few moments then came down to land beside the truck. Miles Mayhem got out and stood talking to a few of his thugs. He broke off when a seaplane came into view.

'Here's one of our first customers,' he said with a smirk.

The seaplane dipped down and skimmed across the surface of the water in a shower of foam. When it stopped, it floated in towards the dock itself.

Mayhem and his men walked over to the edge of the water to await the arrival of the aircraft. The evil genius behind VENOM seemed very satisfied with the way that things were going.

But then he could not see Scott and T-Bob.

They climbed out of the truck and peered cautiously around the dock. Scott turned to the robot to congratulate him.

'Your tracking system actually worked, T-Bob.'

'That surprised me as well,' confessed his friend.

'We gotta find a radio,' insisted the boy.

'Why?'

'So that we can call my Dad.'

'There's no radio around here, Scott.'

'There must be.'

'I don't see it.'

Scott looked all around and then his gaze settled on Switchblade which was standing nearby. A slow smile spread over his face. T-Bob realised what the boy was thinking.

He shook his domed head vigorously.

'No, Scott. No, no, no, no!'

'Yes, T-Bob. Yes, yes, yes, yes!'

'You're crazy!'

'I know.'

'Have you thought what they might do to us if we're caught?'

'We won't be caught.'

'Scott, it's *dangerous,*' argued the robot.

'No,' replied the boy. 'What Hondo MacLean did for me – *that* was dangerous. This is just fun.'

'Fun!!!'

'I need you to distract 'em, T-Bob. Get going.'

The robot began to shake with fright.

SIX

Scott Trakker ran out from behind the truck and headed for Switchblade. T-Bob did his best to divert attention from the boy. The robot rolled towards Mayhem and his thugs on the edge of the dock. He pretended to cry and emitted a high-pitched sobbing.

'Boohoo! Boohoo!'

They did not notice him at first. The seaplane had now come right up to the dock. An evil-looking man climbed out of the cockpit and spoke in a rough, gravelly voice.

'We meet again, Mayhem.'

'Do you have the money?' asked the VENOM leader.

'I got the money if you got the Deathstone.'

T-Bob had now rolled right up to them.

'Excuse me!'

Mayhem and his sidekicks swung round to glare down at the robot. He was fidgeting and trembling and rattling with fear.

'Do you know what time the next bus to Denver will be coming this way?' said T-Bob, in a quavering voice.

The man from the seaplane was very annoyed.

'Is this your idea of a joke, Mayhem?'

'No . . . I, uh . . . well . . .'

'Our negotiations were supposed to be secret!'

'Of course . . . and, you see . . . uh . . .'

'Sorry to butt in,' apologised T-Bob.

Mayhem stared down at him with his bushy eyebrows meeting.

'Who are you?' he demanded.

'Me?' asked T-Bob. 'Oh, I'm nobody!'

'Grab him!' ordered the VENOM chief.

Two thugs seized a metallic arm each and lifted the robot off the ground. T-Bob started to rattle even louder. He was quaking in terror now. He had walked straight into the hands of the enemy.

But he had also performed a valuable service.

Scott Trakker had been able to reach Switchblade unseen and climb into the helicopter. A bank of complex equipment faced him but what caught his eye was an electronic map. Three red dots were blinking on the map in different locations.

'Oh, wow!' he exclaimed.

He reached for the transmitter, held it to his mouth,

then pressed a button on the dashboard. There was a faint crackle.

'Scott to MASK! Scott to MASK! Come in, MASK!'

He waited anxiously for a reply.

The MASK vehicles were speeding in single file down a dirt road. Rhino had sensitive radar antennae and he soon picked up the call.

Alex Sector contacted Matt on the intercom.

'Matt! I've got Scott on the radio.'

'Where is he?'

'Spying on VENOM.'

'Does he want to get himself killed?' said Matt in alarm.

'Hold on,' warned Alex. 'The kid is doing just great. He's given us the map co-ordinates where the meteor fragments are to be sold!'

'But how did he get those?'

'Sheer persistence, I guess.'

'Patch me in, Alex. I want to speak to him.'

'Sure thing, Matt.'

Alex Sector flicked a switch to make it possible.

'Scott!' said Matt. 'Can you hear me?'

'Yeah, Dad.'

'Are you okay, son?'

'I'm fine. How are you?'

'Worried sick about you, of course!'

'Relax. I can take care of myself.'

'Find your way back to the house,' ordered Matt.

'If you say so.'

'I do, Scott. Ask directions if you have to. Okay?'

'I'll make it somehow.'

'And be careful.'

'Yes, *sir*!' replied the boy. 'MASK agent, Scott Trakker, over and out!'

Matt could not suppress a smile.

The boy was indeed an important agent on this mission.

T-Bob, meanwhile, was being questioned by Miles Mayhem and his thugs. Mayhem's deep voice chilled the robot to his innermost circuit.

'What do you know about MASK?' demanded the VENOM leader.

'MASK?'

'That's what I said! Now, don't play tricks with me.'

'I don't know anyone called MASK,' explained T-Bob, shuddering. 'I used to know somebody called Marvin but he doesn't live around here any more. Sorry. Don't ask about MASK.'

'Shake the truth out of him!' snarled Mayhem.

The two thugs began to shake the robot violently.

While this was going on, Scott was experimenting with various switches and levers on the Switchblade control panel. He heaved a sigh.

'Boy! I wish I knew how to fly this thing!'

He pushed a button and Switchblade came alive.

'Go easy now!' shouted the boy. 'Slow down!'

But the helicopter paid no heed. With its blades rotating and its engine roaring, it bounced across the

ground in a series of kangaroo hops. It was now completely out of control and all that Scott could do was to hang on for dear life.

The people on the dock began to panic.

'Say, what's going on, Mayhem?' demanded the man from the seaplane.

'I wish I knew!'

'It's coming straight at us!'

'Look out!' warned Mayhem.

The thugs were so frightened that they let go of T-Bob and the robot was able to roll away to safety. Miles Mayhem was red with fury when he saw that his helicopter had been commandeered. He held up a big hand like a traffic policeman.

'Stop!' he bellowed. 'Stop, Switchblade!'

But the machine came relentlessly on.

Scott pressed, pulled and grabbed everything on the control panel but it made no difference. Switchblade hopped and hopped.

'Help!' cried the boy.

'Switch it off!' suggested T-bob, waving his arms.

'I don't know how to!'

Switchblade was now almost at the water's edge. It pushed Mayhem and the others further and further back towards the lake. Their protests were loud and angry.

'Get back!'

'Cut it out!'

'What are you playing at?'

'Switchblade has gone crazy!'

'It's gonna run us down!' shouted Mayhem.

'We've had it!'

'There's no way out!'

'Stop!!!!'

'AAAAAH!'

Mayhem, his thugs and the man from the seaplane had got right to the very edge of the dock now. As Switchblade made one more leap in the air, they jumped backwards into the water to escape. There was a big splash and they bobbed about in the lake.

The helicopter stopped at the water's edge with one of its landing rails hanging precariously over the dock. Scott did not wait for it to topple in after the others.

Jumping out of the cockpit, he scampered across to a truck.

T-Bob was waiting for him and gave him a welcoming nod.

'Well done! You rescued me!'

'I need to rescue both of us now.'

'Suits me fine.'

'Do you know how to drive this truck?'

'Uh, well . . . you see . . .'

'Great! You get behind the wheel.'

They climbed into the cab of the truck with T-Bob in the driving seat. He switched on the ignition and started to fiddle with the gear lever. The truck backfired a few times then began to jerk wildly from side to side. It went into reverse, stopped, jerked again, then moved slowly forward.

Its gears were grinding dreadfully but it was going.

Scott and T-Bob were making good their escape.

'Where are we making for?' asked the robot.

'The meteor.'

'But the meteor is in three different parts.'

'So? We go in three different directions.'

'At the same time!'

'The way you're driving, T-Bob,' said Scott with a laugh, '*anything* is possible.'

The truck continued to lurch and bounce along.

MASK transports were now on the move with a vengeance. They surged along a desolate road that led to a rocky canyon. When they came to a fork, they split up automatically.

Thunder Hawk converted to a jet and flew straight ahead.

Gator and Firecracker took the right fork while Rhino and Condor chose the left. Each man had a special reason for wanting to get back at VENOM.

Matt Trakker spelled it out for them.

'Okay, gentlemen, this one's for Hondo!'

'You bet!' agreed Brad Turner.

Condor was now driving alongside Rhino but Brad wanted extra speed so that he could get to the enemy as soon as possible. He gave a curt order.

'Switch to laser-guided jet mode!'

Two laser beams shot out from either side of the motorcycle. Between Condor's handlebars was a control panel and Brad now punched some buttons beneath a small video screen. On the screen was a video game-type road created by the laser beams with an animated version of Condor following it.

Brad Turner punched another button.

'Condor to Mach One!'

The bike zoomed away at such mind-boggling speed that it left a blur of itself in its wake. Driving with daredevil skill, Brad took his machine along the treacherously winding road with the twin lasers giving him a terrific thrust.

All danger was ignored.

He was in a hurry.

The small airstrip stood in the middle of the desert. It was flanked by a hangar and a huddle of outbuildings. An aeroplane was standing on the runway and it was guarded by armed thugs. Alongside it was a familiar VENOM machine – Jackhammer.

Cliff Dagger was talking to a dark, sinister, well-dressed man who had just got out of the plane with a briefcase in his hand. In Dagger's own hand was a black, metallic box.

Some kind of deal was obviously taking place.

They were just about to exchange the briefcase for the box when they heard the noise of Condor approaching. Dagger and the man stood open-mouthed in amazement as the motorcycle tore down the runway at supersonic speed and drove straight between them.

Brad Turner gave a triumphant laugh.

'Like taking candy from a baby!'

He had grabbed the black box as he shot past and knocked the briefcase high into the air. The case now opened and millions of dollars began to rain down. The thugs jumped for joy and started to grab at the notes as they fluttered down.

Cliff Dagger looked after the fleeing Condor.

'That was a big mistake, pal!' he warned.

Jackhammer was soon tearing after the motorcycle. Dagger climbed into the turret so that he was ready to fire when he got within range. He wanted to obliterate Condor.

Brad Turner was guiding Condor in and out of

various obstacles. The hangar then loomed up in front of him and there was no way that he could avoid it. He was unruffled.

'Anti-matter comes in handy sometimes,' he noted.

He fired the nose cannon's anti-matter ray at the side of the hangar and created a hole in the wall. Condor sped through it and began to dodge the boxes and equipment it found inside the building.

Dagger urged his vehicle on.

'Come on, VENOM. Get closer!'

Jackhammer headed straight for the hole in the wall but it was not quite big enough to admit the larger vehicle. There was a resounding crash as Jackhammer widened the hole by sheer force. It swerved in and out of the crates and started to close on Condor.

'I've got you now, pal!' sneered Dagger.

But Brad Turner had other ideas. As the other wall of the hangar raced at him, he fired another anti-matter beam and the metal structure dematerialised at once. Condor went out through the new exit and saw a friend waiting for him.

It was Bruce Sato in Rhino.

'He's all yours, Bruce!' said Brad.

His colleague hit a switch on the Rhino dashboard.

'Smokescreen on!'

Jackhammer now ploughed its way through the wall of the hangar and bore down on Rhino. Its front grille and pop-up turrets started firing rapidly but its target soon disappeared.

Thick, black smoke billowed from Rhino's

smokestacks. It was a most effective camouflage. Jackhammer was caught up in the smoke and vanished from sight.

There was a screeching of brakes, then a loud crash.

Dagger howled with homicidal rage.

When the smoke cleared, Jackhammer was nowhere to be seen. Then a hydraulic lift began to rise slowly from the ground with dozens of crates on it. Jackhammer had driven into the hole and landed in the middle of the freight.

The crates were being brought up from underground storage.

They contained chickens.

Thousands of them were now clucking and pecking and flapping their wings. Dagger was completely immersed by feathers. There were even chickens sitting on his mask.

'Get off!' he yelled. 'Go on. Fly away!'

There was a final indignity.

One of the chickens laid an egg in his hand.

SEVEN

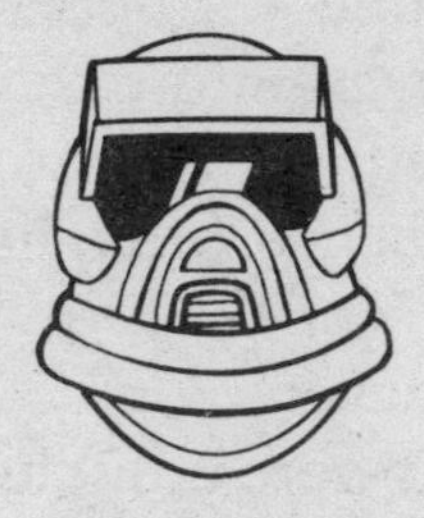

The beach was a popular resort on the Californian coast. It was filled with rich sunbathers, enjoying the sun, sand and surf. Small yachts scudded across the bay. Everyone was having fun.

Then Piranha came speeding along the beach.

People watched in astonishment as it got to the water's edge and launched its submarine-sidecar. Seconds later, the audience had an even bigger shock. Gator came screaming over the sand and skidded to a halt on the shoreline.

Wearing his mask, Dusty Hayes stood up in the jeep and spoke to a pretty young girl in a bikini. Her eyes stared in wonder at him.

'Scuse me, Ma'am. Uh, which way did he go?'

The girl pointed silently towards the ocean.

'Thank ya, kindly!'

Gator converted to a hydroplane and hit the water.

A large yacht was moored some way off. The one-man submarine surfaced beside it and Sly Rax emerged from his Piranha with a black, metallic box in his hand. A big man, wearing a knit cap and sunglasses came out of the cabin on the yacht. He held a briefcase.

'You ready to deal?' asked Rax.

'Yeah. Gimme the Deathstone.'

'Gimme the money first.'

Before they could exchange anything, however, the

hydroplane came hurtling across the surface of the water. Both men were taken aback. Their faces darkened with malice.

'Freeze!' ordered Dusty Hayes.

'Who is that guy?' asked the man on the yacht.

'Ignore him!' advised Rax, anxious to complete the deal.

'Let's trade, then. Quick!'

The man leaned over the rail to pass his briefcase down. Rax lifted the black box up so that the exchange could be made.

Dusty Hayes had to stop them somehow.

'When I say freeze, I mean *freeze*!' he warned.

He shot a water cannon at the two men. A powerful burst of water hit them and then froze into a block of solid ice. Rax and the man on the yacht were locked inside the ice but the black box was held just outside it.

Dusty snatched the box from the hand of the VENOM agent.

'I'll take that, pardner!'

Rax could not speak but his eyes smouldered with hate.

'You all stay cool now, ya hear!' said Dusty.

With a loud whoop, he turned the hydroplane around and raced back towards the shore. His mission had been successful.

Two black boxes had now been recovered.

Two pieces of the meteor were now safe.

One more to go.

Thunder Hawk had converted back to jet mode and was closing in on the lakeside dock. Matt Trakker was at the controls. Hondo MacLean, still very weak, was lying on the stretcher across the back seat. As they approached the dock, the seaplane powered its way across the water and took to the air, leaving a shower of foam in its wake.

Matt realised what must have happened.

'They've already made the transfer. I've got to stop that seaplane somehow.'

'You can do it, Matt,' whispered Hondo.

'I'll circle round and cut them off!'

There was only one problem.

VENOM.

Switchblade was now sitting on Thunder Hawk's tail.

Miles Mayhem chuckled to himself and fired both wings' cannons. The bullets whistled very close to the MASK aircraft. He adjusted his aim and fired another burst at his mortal enemy.

'Looks like we've got company!' said Matt.

'Can you shake him off?' asked Hondo, weakly.

'I'll try.'

Thunder Hawk streaked downwards and flew across the water only metres from the surface. Switchblade was equal to the manoeuvre and stayed right behind. The two jets flashed across the lake then rose to clear the buildings around the dock.

A stand of trees now appeared ahead of them.

Instead of climbing above them, Matt Trakker stayed low and threaded his way down the avenue, his wing tips brushing the leaves. It was a brilliant piece of flying but it still did not dislodge Mayhem in the chasing Switchblade.

'Hold tight, Hondo!' warned Matt.

'Okay!'

As Thunder Hawk emerged from the trees, it went into a steep climb and did a complete loop. By the time that Switchblade was clear of the trees, it found itself with the MASK aircraft on its tail.

'Nice move, Matt,' gasped Hondo.

'Here comes one that's even nicer!'

Thunder Hawk accelerated until it was directly

above Switchblade. Matt judged his position to the last second and then took action.

'Releasing remote-control neutraliser!'

Thunder Hawk released a bomb which landed intact on Switchblade and stuck magnetically to it. The VENOM craft was now carrying the source of its own destruction.

'Bullseye!' said Matt.

'Well . . . done . . .'

The excitement had tired Hondo out and he became unconscious.

Matt Trakker pushed some buttons on his control panel to detonate the bomb. Its rear section fired a rocket burst that was strong enough to override Switchblade's own rockets. The VENOM craft went out of control and careered madly through the sky.

Miles Mayhem clung on desperately to his seat.

'You'll pay for this, MASK!' he threatened.

'Have a pleasant trip, Mayhem,' shouted Matt.

'Arrrgh!'

The VENOM leader yelled in fear as Switchblade began to loop the loop then dive crazily all over the place. MASK had got the upper hand yet again.

But there was one big disappointment.

'That seaplane has got away,' admitted Matt. 'We'll never find it now. And we'll never find that meteor fragment.'

He looked over his shoulder.

'How are you feeling now, Hondo?' Matt was hor-

rified to see that his agent was unconscious. 'Sorry. I'll get you back fast!'

Thunder Hawk turned for home and screamed off.

The MASK transports rendezvoused at the Boulder Hill Gas Station. They drove on to the elevated platform in the garage and were slowly lowered down to the underground headquarters. Matt and his agents made straight for the laboratory. Buddie Hawkes and Alex Sector carried Hondo MacLean on his stretcher and put him down on a table.

Brad Turner held up his black box.

'Here's one piece of the meteor!'

Dusty Hayes pulled out the box he had taken from Rax.

'And here's the second piece. All we need is the third one from Matt and we may have a chance of saving Hondo.'

Matt Trakker's face fell and his shoulders sagged.

'I don't have it, Dusty,' he confessed. 'I failed.'

Professor Stevens, standing nearby, frowned with concern.

'But we must have all *three* segments of the meteor.'

'Is there no other way of saving Hondo?' asked Alex.

'I'm afraid not,' decided the scientist.

The agents were shocked at this news. After all the

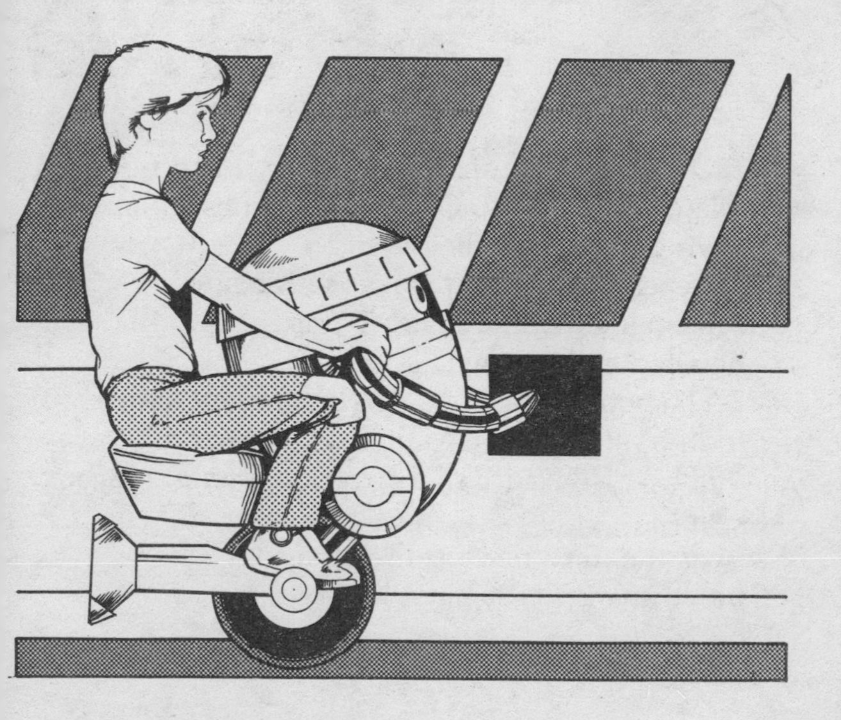

effort they had put into the mission, it had not been completely successful. One of their finest colleagues was dying in front of their eyes.

A screech of tyres and brakes was heard.

Scott Trakker entered with T-Bob.

They had a black, metallic box.

'Hey!' shouted the boy. 'Anybody want a meteor?'

'You've *got* it?' asked Matt in amazement.

'Watch this, Dad,' said Scott, opening the box. 'Ta-daa!'

It was the third piece of the meteor.

The other agents cheered loudly.

Matt grinned. 'I don't know whether to hug you or spank you!'

Professor Stevens touched his elbow.

'Hondo needs immediate attention, Mr Trakker,' she said. 'Could I conduct my experiment, please?'

Everything was set up very quickly. There was a mirrored wall in the laboratory and the three segments of the meteor were placed against it on a metal table. Professor Stevens sat at a control panel. Matt and his agents watched the joining process with her through a reinforced window.

Robot arms descended from the ceiling to grasp the two outside pieces of meteor. They pushed firmly in towards the central segment. There was a spectacular

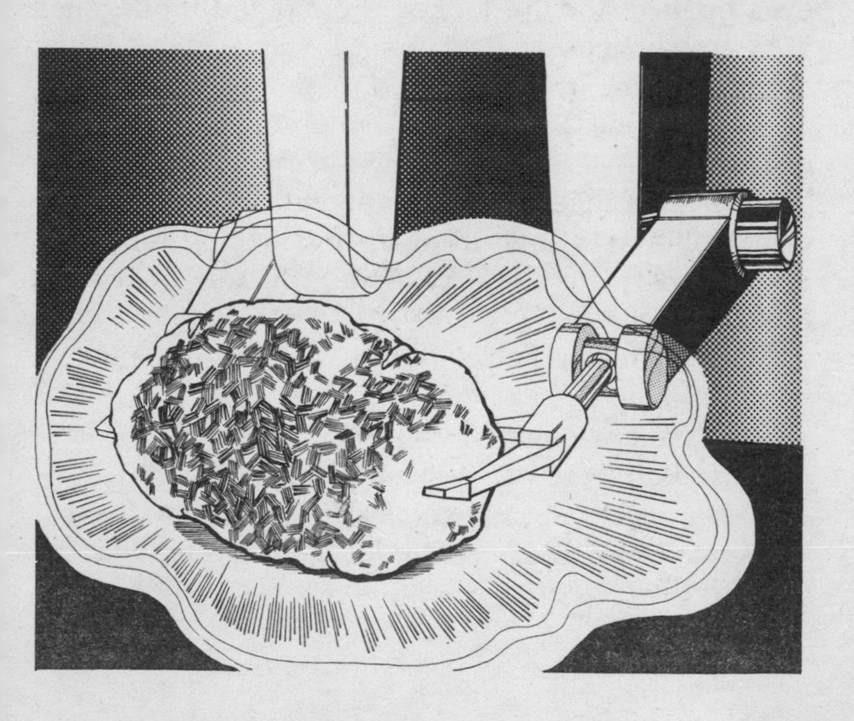

burst of colour and sparks went everywhere. The three segments stopped glowing with the red aura that spelled destruction. They now pulsated with blue-coloured energy.

The life-giving properties had returned.

Wearing a radiation suit, Matt brought Hondo MacLean in on a wheeled stretcher and placed him alongside the meteor. Professor Stevens was very anxious about the agent.

'Did his getting hurt have anything to do with me?'

'That doesn't make any difference, Professor,' replied Matt. 'He just needs your help.'

'He's got it!' she said.

Hondo's body was now bathed in a blue aura. His eyes opened and he looked around the room. His voice was hoarse.

'Hey, where am I?' he asked.

'You've done it, Professor!' congratulated Matt.

'Hurrah!'

The agents cheered and jumped up and down with glee. Hondo was now sitting up and looking as if he'd made a complete recovery. The Professor smiled at Matt Trakker.

'Thank you for helping me,' she said. 'MASK is wonderful.'

'Looks like we helped each other, Professor,' Matt replied. 'You were pretty wonderful yourself.'

'I was just doing my job,' she added, modestly. 'And right now that job includes figuring out what to do with the meteor.'

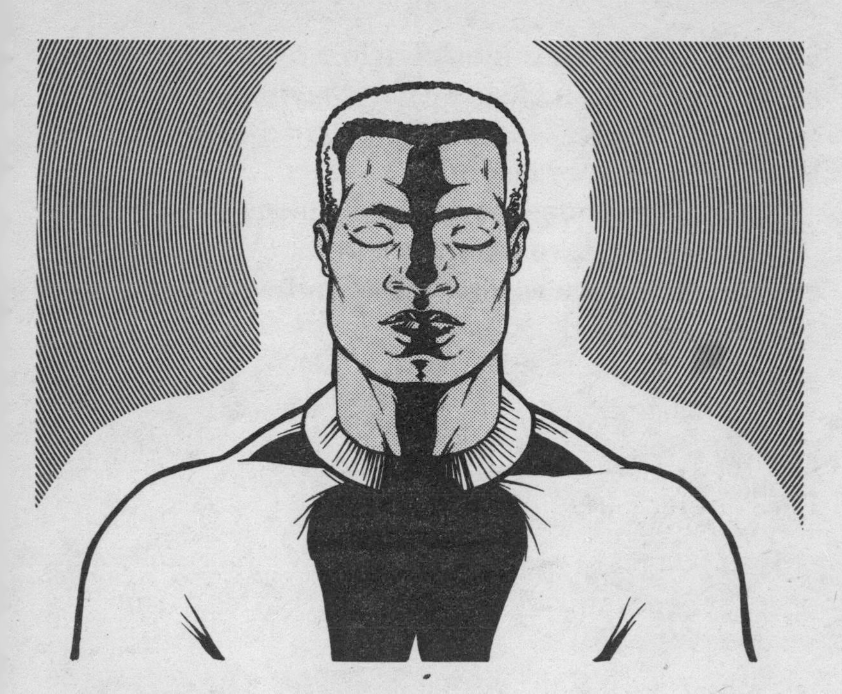

'I don't think we'll have to do anything with it,' noted Matt. 'Take a look at it.'

Professor Stevens stared at the meteor and saw what he meant. It had stopped glowing altogether and was giving off no radiation at all.

Dusty Hayes slapped his thigh and whooped.

'Well, I'll be!' he yelled. 'The dang thing don't work any more. Boy! They sure don't make meteors like they used to!'

Professor Stevens joined in the laughter with Matt Trakker and his agents. Scott and T-Bob laughed the loudest of all.

The Deathstone had died.

Switchblade finally came down in a remote part of the desert. A dazed and angry Miles Mayhem got out and spoke to Dagger and Rax who had parked their VENOM machines nearby.

Mayhem pounded his fist on the side of his aircraft.

'MASK may have won the battle but the war goes on! Next time, the victory will be mine!'

Or so he hoped.

Get ready for a second MASK adventure: MASK 2 – Peril Under Paris